To the sweet dreamers . . . Madeleine, Augustin, Robinson, Marilou, Samuel, Aurélie, Achille, Alexandre.

Thanks to the French National Museum of Natural History for their friendly fact-checking.

First published in the United States in 2019
by Eerdmans Books for Young Readers,
an imprint of Wm. B. Eerdmans Publishing Co.
4035 Park East Court SE, Grand Rapids, Michigan 49546
www.eerdmans.com/youngreaders

Originally published in France in 2017 under the title *Doux Rêveurs*
by Éditions courtes et longues, Paris
© Éditions courtes et longues, 2017
English-language translation © 2019 Sarah Ardizzone

27 26 25 24 23 22 21 20 19          1 2 3 4 5 6 7 8 9

ISBN 978-0-8028-5517-6

A catalog listing is available from the Library of Congress.

The illustrations were created digitally.

Isabelle Simler

# SWEET DREAMERS

Eerdmans Books for Young Readers

Grand Rapids, Michigan

Slung like a hammock,
the sloth dreams
of spring-loaded sprinters,
of rockets blasting off,
of pump-action spinning tops.
When the stopwatch starts,
our dreaming racer
doesn't move
an inch.

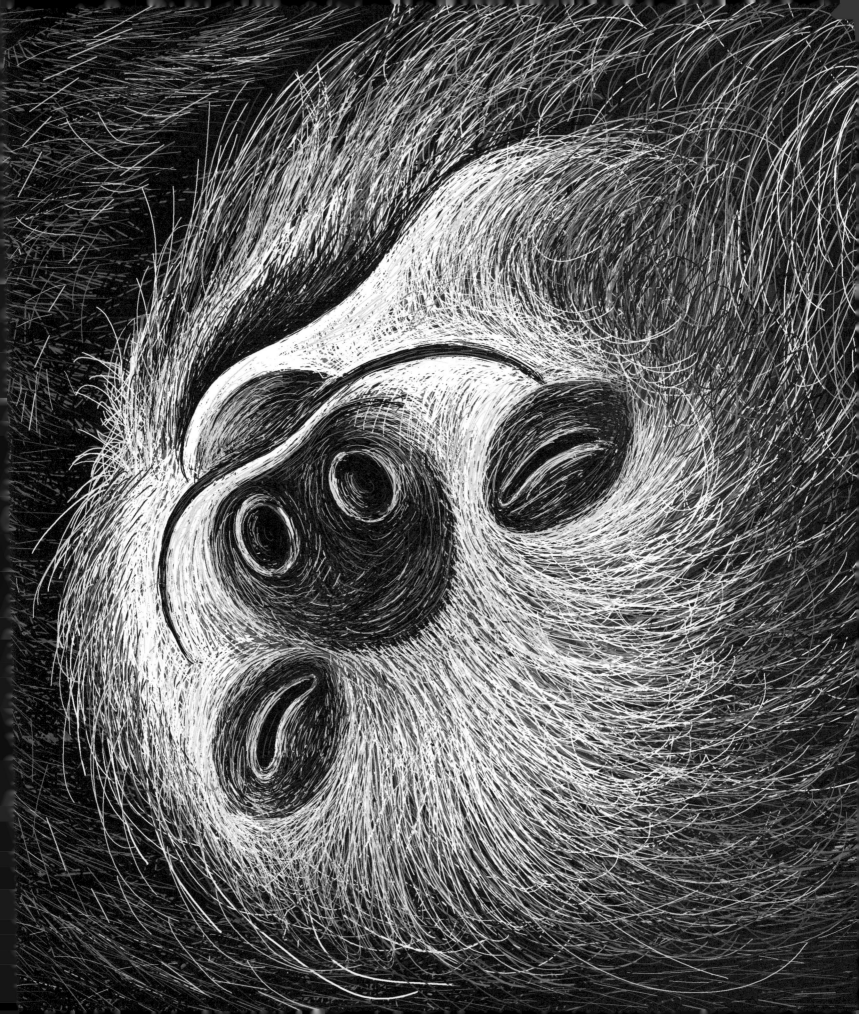

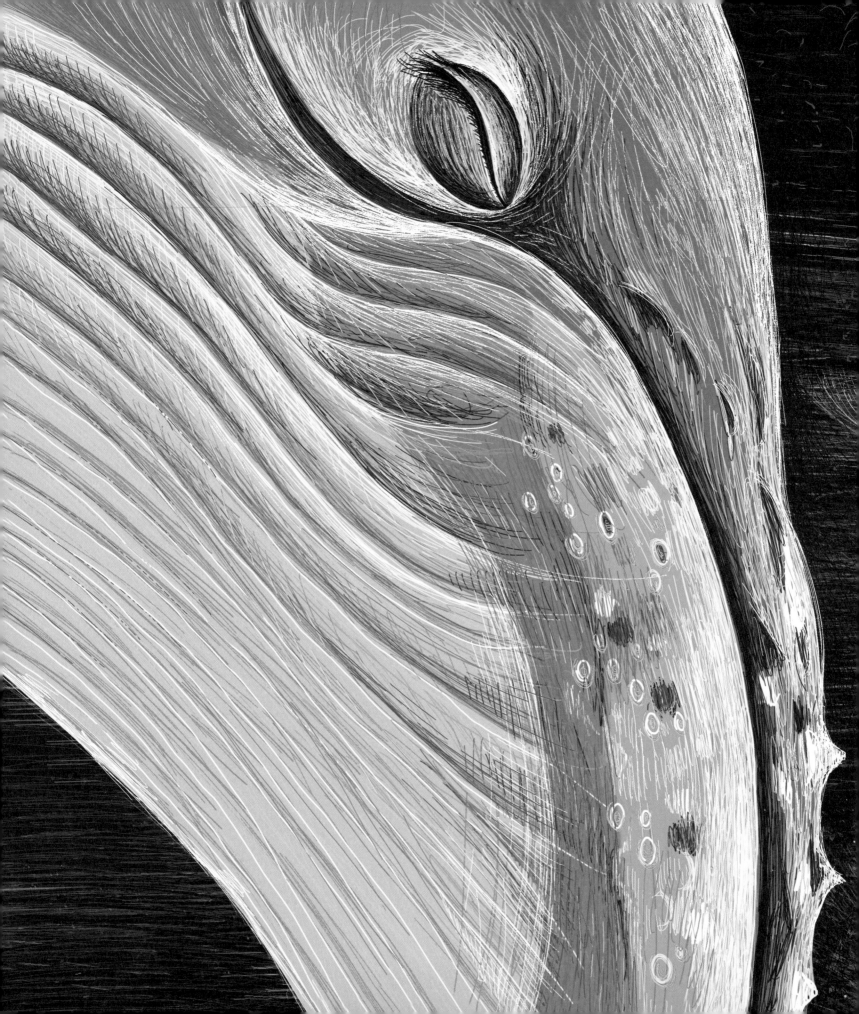

The humpback whale
dreams vertically,
with plankton at every level.
Balancing on her head
or the tip of her tail,
this ballerina nosedives
into sleep.

Bundled into a ball,
the red-breasted robin
dreams of spring.
Icy beak tucked inside scarlet feathers,
he remembers the taste of blueberries, blackcurrants, and cherries.

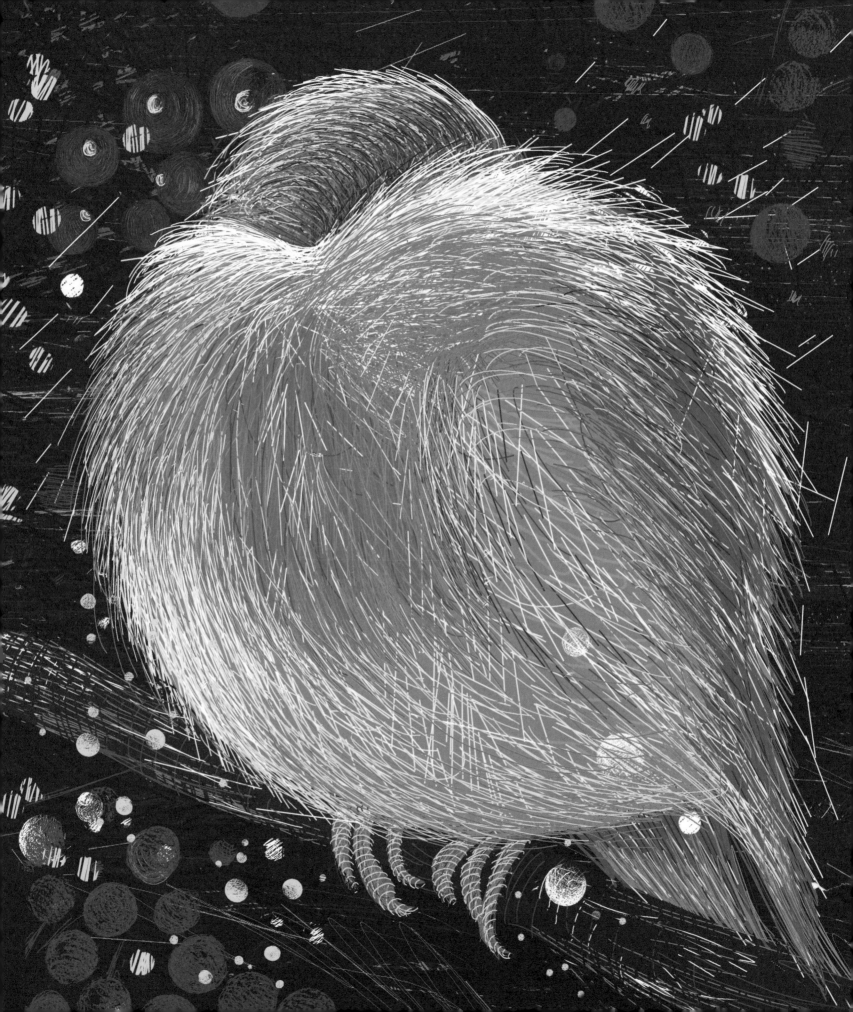

Toes clinging to the ceiling,
kite-fingers folded like a blanket,
**the bat dreams upside down.**
As the day shines, she slips into darkness.

The hedgehog dreams
safely in his shelter.
Under a pile of leaves,
in his spiky coat,
he's rolled up, wrapped up
for a long rest.

The swallow dreams in full flight,
wings outstretched as the breezes carry her.
Feathers in the wind,
beak in the air,
she dozes lightly, so lightly.

As if wrapped in silk
with shrimp-tinted reflections,
she slides her delicate head
between her feathers.
The flamingo dreams in pink.

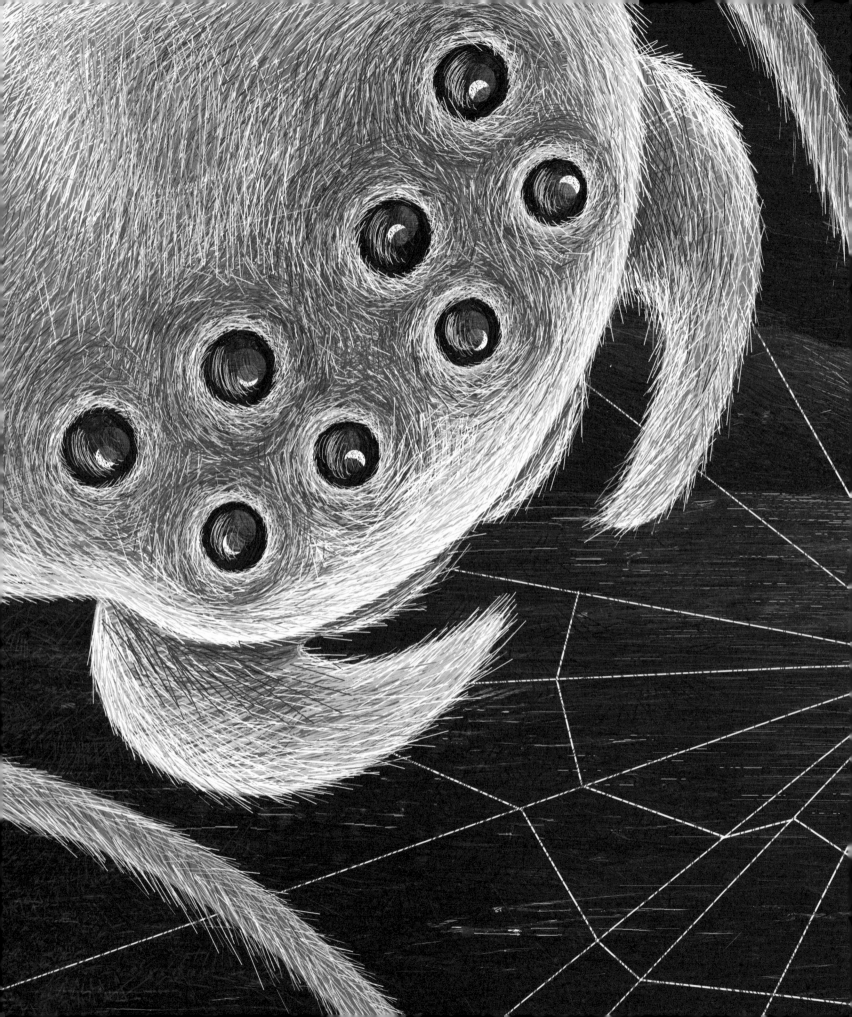

Eight legs to stand on,
eight moons mirrored in his eyes,
**the spider dreams on a tightrope—**
the lacework pattern of his sleep
hanging by a thread.

Her heart slows
in the riverbed.
Her legs get bogged down
as she sinks even lower.
The frog dreams in the mud.

The ant gathers
and collects
hundreds of quick naps.
Asleep in his colony,
he dreams of dots
marching in single file.

Tight inside his twisting shell,
the snail stretches
to the bottom of his bed.
**His dreams spiral out.**

Even as she dreams,
the cat is on the lookout.
At the rustle of a leaf,
her ears twitch.
At the beating of a wing,
her whiskers quiver.
She purrs herself back to sleep again.

Afraid of nothing,
his belly full,
**the lion dreams in peace.**

**The elephant dreams in granite.**
Her trunk unfurls,
her legs take root.
Planted by a heavy drowsiness,
the great animal slumbers.

Beneath her long eyelashes,
the giraffe enjoys graceful dreams.
This elastic giant
leaves the acacia trees
to fold herself
into a slender snooze.

The koala dreams
in a canopy of branches.
Full belly against cool bark,
his silvery fur
hugs the eucalyptus.

With an electric swish
and a butterfly silhouette,
the stingray dreams under the sand,
lurking with powdery wings.

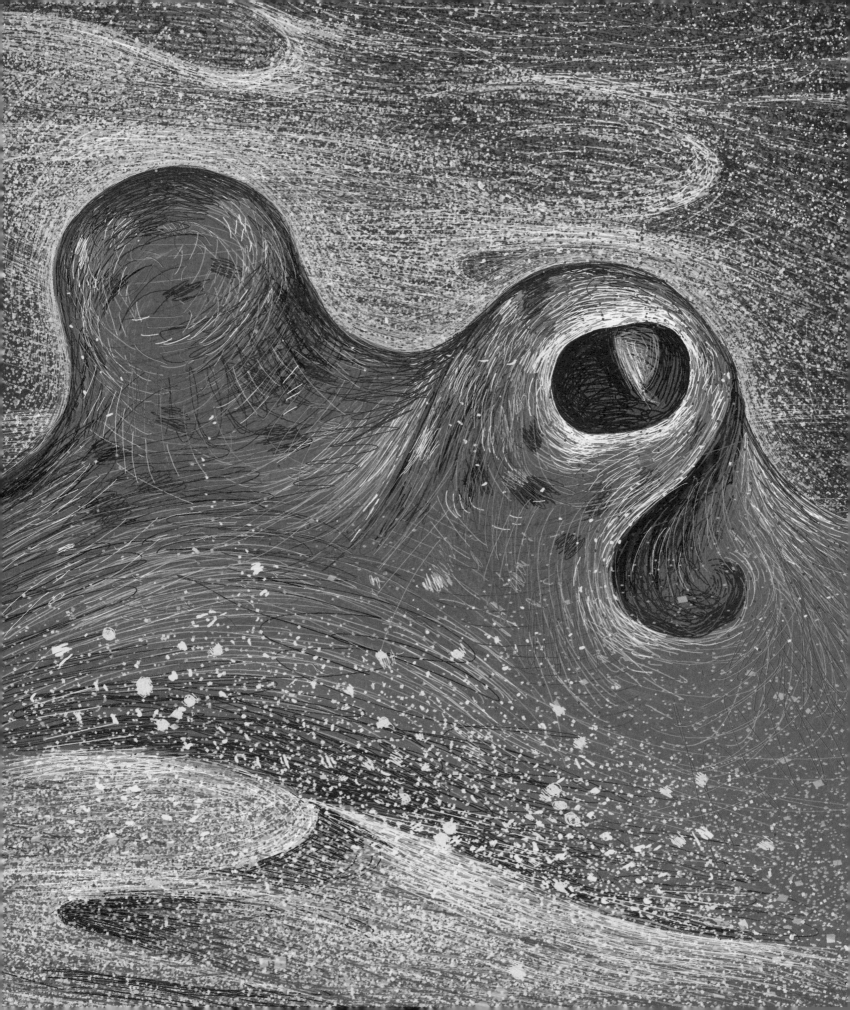

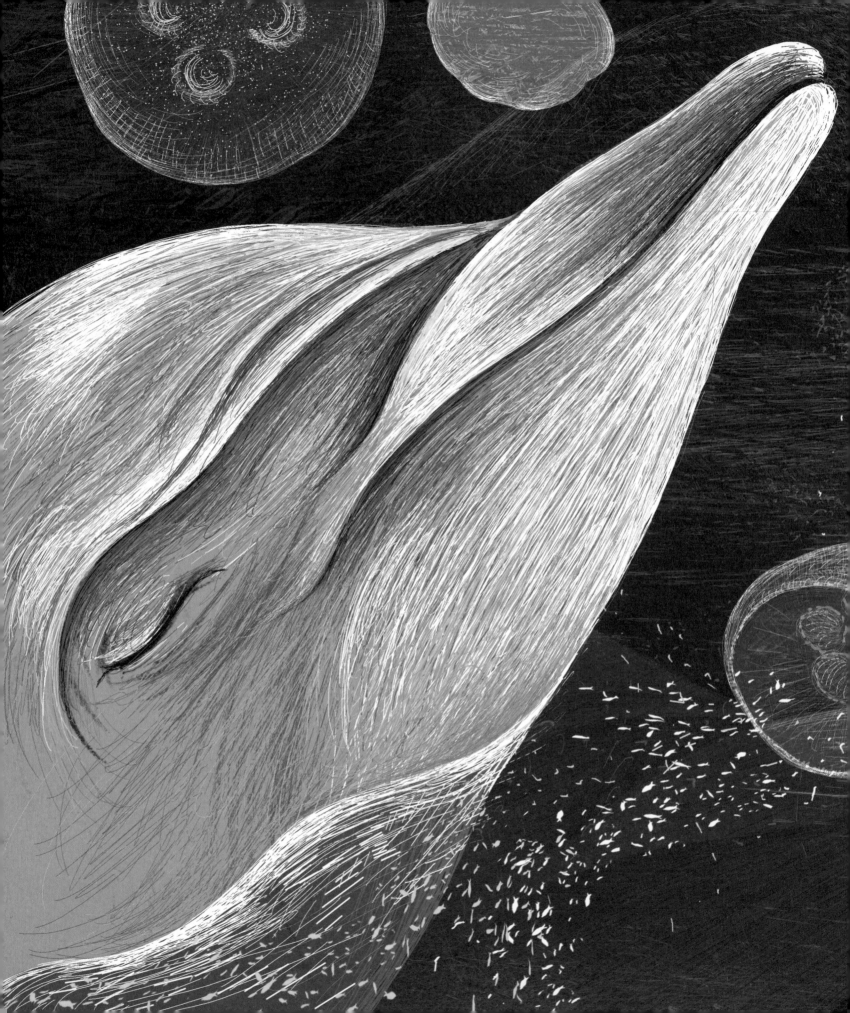

One eye open, the other shut,
**the dolphin only half-dreams.**
Her yawn skims the water
as she part-sleeps, part-swims
among the jellyfish.

He clings to a stalk
and drifts with the waves.
As if on a carousel,
the seahorse dreams at a gallop.

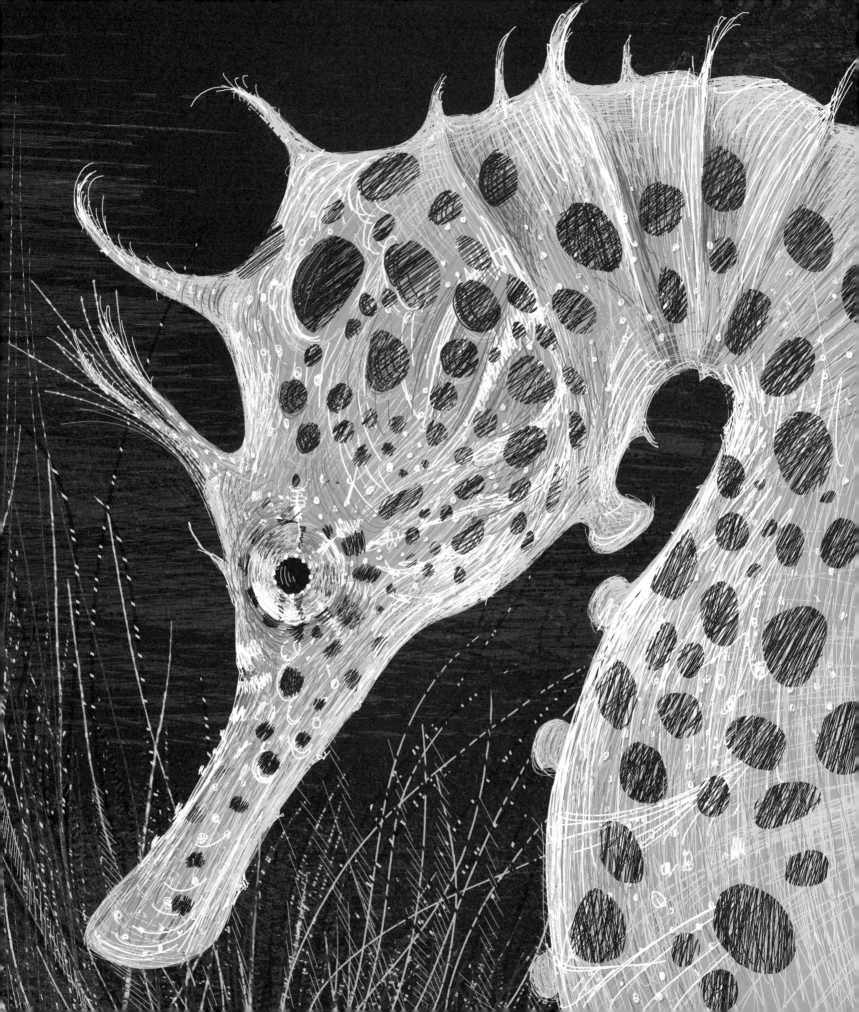

She settles on a rock,
mimics a pebble,
and sleeps like a stone.
The octopus dreams in disguise.

The wolf dreams in the forest
at the foot of a great oak tree.
His piercing eyes slowly close
as he lies on his bed of cool grass.

Puffing up her feathers
in a quilted hollow,
the grouse dreams under the snow.
She spends the night in secret
beneath that great white sheet.

The squirrel dreams
in the hollow of a tree.
Inside his nest of feathers and moss,
he wraps his tail around him
and counts hazelnuts as he drifts off to sleep.

The rabbit hops inside his burrow
and vanishes into the maze.
He dreams far below the grass,
snug in his dug-out bedroom.

The horse dreams standing up,
in the middle of the herd.
She never loses her footing,
although her thoughts break free.

Four cloven hooves at the base of a stump,
warm breath between his tusks.
The wild boar dreams among the brambles,
his snout buried in bracken.

The firefly flashes as she dreams
in the long grass.
When she shoots off into the night,
this winged beetle sparkles like a star.

She clambers onto the whale,
straddles the seahorse,
clings to the elephant,
swoops with the swallow.
All night long, cuddling her koala,
**the child dreams beneath the moon.**